SUPER HAPPY PARTY BEARS

STAYING A HIVE

STAYING A HIVE

MARCIE
COLLEEN

[Imprint]
MAKE YOUR MARK

NEW YORK

{Imprint}
MAKE YOUR MARK

A part of Macmillan Children's Publishing Group,
a division of Macmillan Publishing Group, LLC

SUPER HAPPY PARTY BEARS: STAYING A HIVE.
Copyright © 2017 by Imprint. All rights reserved. Printed in China
by Toppan Leefung Printing Ltd., Dongguan City, Guangdong Province.
For information, address Imprint, 175 Fifth Avenue, New York, N.Y. 10010.

Library of Congress Cataloging-in-Publication Data is available.
ISBN 978-1-250-10047-4 (paperback) / ISBN 978-1-250-10048-1 (ebook)
Our books may be purchased in bulk for promotional, educational,
or business use. Please contact your local bookseller or the Macmillan
Corporate and Premium Sales Department at (800) 221-7945 ext. 5442
or by e-mail at MacmillanSpecialMarkets@macmillan.com.

Book design by Christine Kell
Imprint logo designed by Amanda Spielman
Illustrations by Steve James

First Edition—2017

1 3 5 7 9 10 8 6 4 2

mackids.com

If this book isn't yours, keep your thieving paws off it.
Obey or may every bite of your jelly doughnut be jelly-less.

TO ALL OF THE BEES IN MY HIVE
AND ONE VERY SPECIAL BUG

CHAPTER ONE

Welcome to the Grumpy Woods!

Just kidding. Go away!

In the past, the animals of the Grumpy Woods have given new critters hints that were ignored. First, they built a tall wooden fence to keep out certain bears. Certain bears, meaning the dancing, singing, doughnut-chowing bears. But a bunch of beavers chewed the fence down and used it to build a dam. A very nice one, actually.

Then there was Humphrey Hedgehog's masterpiece: the rock-and-stick Grumpy Wall. Mostly rocks, with a row of sticks along the top. It worked really well to keep out those who follow the laws of gravity. But winged creatures like woodpeckers? That's another story.

So there is a new Mayoral
Decree regarding woodpeckers.
And knock-knock jokes. Neither
are considered funny or welcome
in the Grumpy Woods. The townscritters don't laugh much at all,
because every animal here is, well,
GRUMPY.

If you insist on telling a

knock-knock joke, you'll quickly
find yourself dragged down to City
Hall to face the mayor himself.
Sherry Snake—or Sheriff Sherry, as
she prefers to be called—patrols
these parts along with Squirrelly
Sam. They both like tattling on
those who break the rules.

Mayor Quill's list of Mayoral

Decrees keeps getting longer and longer. He's up to Mayoral Decree 1,235: *Just don't.* Yet rules don't seem to be enough.

Humphrey Hedgehog, the assistant deputy to Mayor Quill, insists that more action is necessary. He wants to build a new wall of pinecones, even

though the first two

walls didn't work.

Squirrelly Sam has

proposed creating a dome over

the Grumpy Woods to seal it off

from the outside world, but when

Bernice Bunny

asked him how

he was going to do

that, he simply stuffed his mouth full of nuts and acted as if he couldn't hear the question.

Bernice Bunny then suggested digging a castle moat around the woods, like in the kingdoms she's read about in her books, but Dawn Fawn pointed out that they didn't have a castle. And that still water attracts mosquitoes.

Needless to say, they haven't agreed on anything yet.

And so, every day, everyone in the Grumpy Woods wakes up

already out of sorts and orders

up some breakfast—a bowl of

"BAAAAHHHH, humbug!" and a

crusty stack of *whoop-dee-doo*.

That is, everyone except the

Super Happy Party Bears.

If you follow the carefully placed sticks, laid out in the shape of arrows, up the flower-lined path, you'll see the welcome sign out front. At the Party Patch, the Headquarters of Fun, life is very different.

LIFE IS SUPER.

Life is happy. And life is full of parties!

And so, on any beautiful morning, the Super Happy Party Bears wake up already smiling and order up some breakfast—a half order of freshly baked exclamation points and a side order of *Yippee skippee*!

Nothing annoys everyone in the Grumpy Woods more.

Except when the bears have a party.

And they are always having a party.

13

CHAPTER TWO

While bees collected pollen from
the cheery flowers outside the
Party Patch, pans clattered and
batter splattered inside. Clouds
of baking flour floated through
the air as the daily doughnut
preparation got into full swing.

Mixers whirred and large spoons stirred to the beat of the Super Happy Party Band's version of "If You're Happy and You Know It." Their all-time favorite verse of the song was "If you're happy and you know it, lick that bowl."

The littlest bear had the
most important job: doughnut
decoration. A dash of powdered
sugar here and a handful of
rainbow sprinkles there.

The doughnuts looked spectacular. He adjusted his chef hat and got ready to embellish the next batch with chocolate frosting stripes.

Ziggy, the front man of the Super Happy Party Band, sang, "If you're happy and you know it, hum a tune," and the littlest bear

hummed along, *hum-hum-hum*. And his hat seemed to hum along with him. Actually, it sounded more like a *buzz-buzz-buzz*.

"Did you hear that?" the littlest bear asked Shades.

Shades peered over his star glasses and asked, "Did I hear what?" Then he jumped back into the song and sang out, "If you're happy and you know it, lick that bowl!"

As the song went on, so did the humming.

The littlest bear then turned to Jacks, who was standing *in* the biggest bowl, kneading dough

by jogging. Jacks's morning dancercise routine was a key part of making the doughnuts.

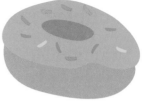

"Excuse me, Jacks, but do you hear buzzing?"

Jacks was too busy counting his reps and remembering to breathe to answer the question.

The buzzing continued. After questioning more bears, the littlest bear finally checked in with Bubs, who was in the corner blowing

bubbles. Bubs always had some
party wisdom to share.

"Mr. Bubs," asked the littlest

bear, "do you happen to hear a buzzing?"

The bubble on the end of Bubs's wand grew and grew as he blew with a steady, calm breath. When the bubble was ready to take flight, Bubs carefully lifted the littlest bear's chef hat to reveal a bee wearing big glasses and happily dancing along to the music. The bubble slowly drifted away, wobbling.

"I have a bee in my bonnet!" cheered the littlest bear. "A new friend!"

When the bee realized he was being watched, he froze.

The music stopped. So did the doughnut making, as all the bears gathered around to see.

"He's so cute!" Jacks said.

"I will call him Stripey," said the littlest bear.

But then Stripey cleared his throat. "Actually, the name's, um, Stan. But seeing as I am in hiding, perhaps a name change would be good for me."

"Stan!" cheered the bears. "Hooray for Stan!"

"Shhhhhhh!" said Stan. "I'm in *hiding*. Remember?"

"Are you a honeybee?" squealed the bears.

"More like a bumble—or *bumbling*—bee," said Stan, pushing his thick glasses up on his nose.

"But are you a *honey*bee?" squealed the bears.

"Yes. I am a honeybee by trade. I'm just not very good at it. You see, I, uh, I have a horrible pollen allergy."

27

Stan sneezed. "It puts a
damper on the whole honey thing.
I get within a few inches of a flower
and I become a drippy-nosed,
red-eyed mess. Trust me, it's not
a happy sight." Stan pulled out a

hankie and blew his nose. "I've begged for a desk job, but the only opening is in sales. I don't know the first thing about selling honey. I mean, how do you even find customers?"

"WE LOVE HONEY!"

cheered the bears.

Suddenly, Stan had an idea.

"Follow me," he said.

CHAPTER THREE

Mayor Quill carefully styled the remaining quills on his head. The truth was, with all the Mayoral Decrees he'd written recently, one quill at a time, the porcupine had a bit of a bald spot. He gently hid the thinning spot with a comb-over and reminded himself to pluck quills for writing new decrees from his rump until the quills grew back.

"You are still a handsome devil," he said to himself.

Just then Humphrey Hedgehog
appeared in the doorway, carrying
Mayor Quill's breakfast tray. "Why,
thank you, sir," said Humphrey,
puffing up his chest. "I have been
working out."

Humphrey carefully set up
Mayor Quill's breakfast just as he
liked it: Juice
to the left.
Spoon to
the right.

Bowl of twigs
and berries
front and
center.
Last but
not least,
Humphrey
placed a napkin,
perfectly folded in
a triangle, under
the spoon and set
a vase of colorful flowers at the
far corner. Believe it or not, even
grumps enjoy flowers.

The mayor heard something. "Mayoral Decree one hundred three," grumbled the mayor. "No humming."

"I wasn't humming," said Humphrey.

Mayor Quill grunted and lumbered over to eat his breakfast.

As the mayor's whole head disappeared into the bowl, Humphrey flipped through the pages on his clipboard in preparation for his morning report. He had learned early on not to interrupt the gobbles and grunts. Quill storms were still possible while the mayor was eating. The hedgehog had discovered that the hard way. And one particular

quill had already escaped the
comb-over and was aimed straight
at Humphrey.

Mayor Quill abruptly stopped eating. "There's that humming again."

"I heard it, too," said Humphrey. "It sounded like a deflating balloon."

"Not at all," said Mayor Quill. "A balloon losing air sounds more like *pfffffttt*."

"True, sir. What I meant to

say is that it sounded like an old whoopee cushion."

"Are you kidding?" responded the mayor. "An old whoopee cushion sounds more like *ffffffffffff*."

"Absolutely, sir. I am not quite sure what I was thinking. It sounded more like someone letting the air out of your car's tires," said Humphrey.

"I don't have a car!" said Mayor Quill through clenched teeth. His fist came pounding down on the desk, toppling over the vase of flowers. A cloud of bees, suddenly disrupted from their pollen collecting, filled the office.

"B-b-b-bees," gulped Humphrey.

"No worries," said Mayor Quill. "They won't bother us if we don't bother them."

Bees buzzed all around for several minutes. The mayor and Humphrey sat still, careful not to move even a single quill.

"The buzzing is actually quite lovely," whispered Humphrey.

"Indeed," said Mayor Quill.

"I feel like a flower."

Just then Squirrely Sam, the Grumpy Woods' nosy forest gossip,

appeared, scrambling down from the branches above.

"Excuse me, Mr. Mayor," he shouted over the hum. A bee landed on Sam's nose.

Sam's eyes crossed to look at the bee. Sam took a deep breath and...

"BEEEEEEEEEEE!"

he screamed as he swatted and swung at the swarm with his bushy tail. "Get it off me! Get it off!"

"This is Squadron Twelve. We're under attack," reported the leader bee into a walkie-talkie. "Activate SWAT team."

The swarm promptly took the
shape of a giant fly swatter and
THWACKED those townscritters
up one grumpy side and down the
other.

CHAPTER FOUR

The woods were abuzz. Overnight,
a hive of bees had moved into the
many holes carved by Wallace
Woodpecker along the Grumpy
Wall. Now they were open for
business. The honey business,
that is.

The Grumpy Wall was hardly recognizable. On both sides, a giant beehive swallowed up the rocks and twigs. Busy bees flew in and out of every crack and hole, now filled with oozing honeycomb.

Stan hesitated and turned to the twelve beaming bears behind him.

"You aren't exactly the delivery Queen Beetrice is expecting, so I need you all to be very quiet and wait here for a minute, until I give you further instructions."

"Like a surprise party?"
whispered the bears.

"Yeah, like a surprise party,"
whispered Stan.

"We love surprise parties!"
cheered the bears.

Stan braced himself as the
cheer echoed through the Grumpy

Woods. But luckily, no one seemed to notice. He wiped his brow and mouthed the words *Okay, stay right here*. The Super Happy Party Bears mouthed the word *Okay*. And gave thumbs-ups. But as Stan turned toward the hive, he caught a bit of pollen in his nose.

ACHOOOOOOOOOOOOOOOOOOO!

Immediately, a swarm of bees appeared. They moved as one and took on the shape of a stop sign.

"Halt right there!" the bees said in unison.

"We've located B-63, Your
Majesty," said one bee into a
walkie-talkie. "He's empty-handed.
We'll bring him in for punishment."
The swarm formed the shape of a
cage around Stan.

"Please, B-1, I can explain," begged Stan, pushing his glasses up on his nose.

"Save it for Queen Beetrice," said B-1 as all the bees swarmed to form the shape of an arrow pointing toward the hive.

The Super Happy Party Bears marveled at the fun shapes. "Oooh! We LOVE charades!"

The swarm stopped.

"Who are you?" the bees asked while taking on the shape of a Super Happy Party Bear.

The bears burst into applause.

"Move along. There is nothing to see here," said the bees, creating the shape of a stern-faced bee.

The bears burst into applause once more.

"Do it again!"

"More! More!"

"Do Quilly next!"

However, the swarm did not listen. Instead, the bees turned their attention back to their prisoner.

"Move it, B-63!"

"Perhaps we should get these lovely customers their honey first," said Stan.

"HONEY!" cheered the bears.

The littlest bear pulled out a loaf of cinnamon bread and started handing out slices. He gave one to each of the bears, who held the bread gently between their paws, at the ready for a huge squeeze of honey.

Just then a crackle came over B-1's walkie-talkie in the form of a very agitated voice. "What is the holdup?"

At the sound of Queen Beetrice's voice, the entire swarm bowed their heads and shoulders. B-1 fumbled and dropped the walkie-talkie. Stan quickly picked the device up and stammered, "Uh, on our way, um, Your Majesty. Just taking care of some, um, of our customers first."

"Customers? It's about time this colony did something right," barked the queen. And then the line when dead.

Stan sheepishly handed the walkie-talkie back to B-1 and left the middle of the swarm. He looked out at the bears.

"So, uh," said Stan, hovering nervously, "who wants honey?"

"WE DO!" cheered the bears.

"Ahem." Stan cleared his throat in the direction of the swarm. "You heard Queen Beetrice. These customers need honey."

The swarm buzzed into action. Three of the bees flew into the

hive and then
returned, hoisting
an enormous spigot
over their heads.

With the help of the rest of the
swarm, who had taken the shape
of a hammer, they drove the
spigot right into the bulging side

of the Grumpy Wall hive. Last, they placed a bucket underneath to catch the honey.

The bears licked their lips as they watched the bees turn the handle of the spigot. Like water from a faucet, honey began to flow. Yet it didn't make it to the bucket. Instead, the line of bears approached, and one by one they held their slices of cinnamon bread under the nozzle. When the bread was gone, they simply drank straight from the tap. They guzzled, gulped, and squeezed every last drop the bees had created.

"Life is a flower of which love is the honey," said Bubs afterward. He lay back on the grass, his fuzzy blue belly round with satisfaction.

"So we just wait here, then?" asked Mops.

"Um, for what?" asked Stan.

"The next batch!" said the littlest bear.

"SUPER HAPPY HONEY TIME! SUPER HAPPY HONEY TIME!"

The entire hive was dry. Not a drop of honey remained.

Stan had created monsters.

CHAPTER FIVE

While the worker bees hurried to replenish the honey, Stan was called into Queen Beetrice's office for a meeting. He sat in the waiting room, pretending to casually flip through this month's copy of *Beedazzled* magazine. Instead, he recited the rules for "if you ever meet the queen" over and over in his head. He had memorized these rules when he was a young bee-ling.

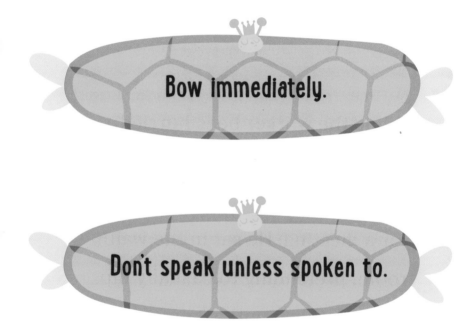

Bow immediately.

Don't speak unless spoken to.

Do not look her in the eye.

"The queen will see you now," announced the security bee at her doorway.

Stan nervously wiped his sticky-honey hands on his belly, took a quick puff on his inhaler, and fluttered through the door.

Inside, the air was cloudy with pollen. Stan could feel his head

stuffing up as he bowed. His nose

began to itch. His eyes began to

tear.

"Why, if it isn't today's hero,"

said Queen Beetrice. "B-63?"

Stan nodded and could feel the congestion in his head shift from side to side as he did.

"What is your real name?" asked the Queen.

It was then that Stan's nose could take no more. He pinched, he squirmed, and he held his breath, but it was no use.

"ACHOOOOOOOOOOOOOO!" he sneezed everywhere.

"Interesting name, Achoo," said Queen Beetrice. "I'll get on with it. I've asked you here because it has become evident that the market is calling for more honey. Do you agree?"

Stan sniffled and nodded.

"What do you propose we do? In your expert opinion, of course," she asked.

This was Stan's big moment. He cleared his throat and pulled out some statistics and charts he had drawn up to show the hive's growing business and future potential.

"Well, Your Majesty, I suppose

we should expand the hive,
ramp up pollen collection and
production, and perhaps install
some conveyor belts."

Queen Beetrice nodded. And
then she frowned.

"I appreciate your thoughts, but

I'll tell you what I propose. We need to expand the hive, ramp up pollen collection and production, and install some conveyor belts," the queen proclaimed.

Stan was silent. Queen Beetrice glared at Stan. It was evident she was waiting for applause, so Stan clapped as loudly as he could.

"Can I count on you, Achoo, to see my plan through?"

"Most definitely, Your Majesty," said Stan.

"Well then, show me the honey!"

she cheered, and gestured for Stan to leave the office.

He bowed and turned to go, happy that he had kept one idea to himself so that no one else could take credit for it.

He was going to design squeezy bottles shaped like the hive's best customers—the Super Happy Party Bears.

CHAPTER SIX

City Hall was all abuzz, too. In the crankiest sort of way. It seemed that Mayor Quill, Humphrey, and Sam were not the only townscritters who had already met the bees, and everyone came to City Hall to complain.

"My sooOOOOthing lavender eye mask is to help me sleep, not attract hooOOOOdlums!" screeched Opal Owl, who had awoken covered from beak to talon in bees.

"Sssticky honey dropssss are making it impossssible to patrol the Grumpy Wall," hissed Sherry, her skin covered in grass and dirt

from slithering in and out of
the honey.

"I can't read with all this
buzzing!" said Bernice Bunny.

"Buzz, buzz, swat, swat, swat!"
sang Dawn Fawn. While she was
busy feather-dusting, she had
stirred up bees who were collecting
pollen in some dandelions. They

thought they
were under
attack and
called in the
SWAT team,
who took
the shape
of a broom.
Normally,

Dawn would have been thrilled to
see such a large cleaning tool, as
she was a fan of a clean sweep, but
she wasn't used to being the one
who was swept away.

Humphrey pouted. "They tried to sting me."

"Enough!" said Mayor Quill. His quills shuddered. "These bees are not only a nuisance; they are a threat to the very life we have here in the Grumpy Woods. They are dangerous and destructive.

We need to let them know that they—and their honey—are not welcome here. By Mayoral Decree one-two-three-six—"

"HONEY FOR EVERYONE!" cheered Sam, finally entering the meeting. In his paw was a golden squeezy bottle. The bottle was shaped like a cheery—or, should we say, super happy—bear.

Mayor Quill stomped his foot. He shook from head to toe. Humphrey rolled into a defensive ball. Quills shot out everywhere. One narrowly missed Sherry, who was unable to move her sticky self fast enough to get out of the way. Another soared straight toward Sam and speared the tummy of the bear bottle. When the storm had passed, Humphrey peeked out.

"Well done, honey," he said. "I mean, sir."

CHAPTER SEVEN

The townscritters marched
straight to the Grumpy Wall.
They were wearing makeshift
beekeeper masks and suits made
out of woven grasses and carefully
placed pinecones—no one wanted
to risk being stung. Mayor Quill

led the way, gripping the mangled and twisted bear bottle in his paw. The others carried protest signs.

"Remember," said Humphrey, "the chant is 'Take Your Honey and Stick It!'"

"But why can't we eat the honey?" asked Sam.

"Eating the honey will only encourage them to stay," explained

Humphrey. "When they realize there is no business here, they are sure to move along."

When they reached the wall, Mayor Quill pulled out his megaphone and boomed, "By Mayoral Decree one-two-three-six—"

"HONEY FOR EVERYONE!"

declared Stan as he popped his head out of the hive.

"YAY!" cheered the bears. "HONEY FOR EVERYONE!"

"That's the best Mayoral Decree ever!" said Jacks. And the bears did their Super Happy Party Dance.

Slide to the right.

Hop to the left.

Shimmy, shimmy, shake.

Strike a pose.

"You can Waggle Dance?" asked Stan.

Immediately, a squadron formed the shape of a compass.

"It's our Super Happy Party Dance," explained Mops. "We do it whenever we are happy."

"Which is most of the time!" Little Puff giggled.

"Do it again," said B-1.

Slide  to the right.

Hop to the left.

Shimmy, shimmy, shake.

 Strike a pose.

"B-5, interpret the coordinates," ordered B-1 as another bee left the formation and did his own version of the dance.

Glide to the right.

Zoom to the left.

Buzz, buzz, flutter.

Point a stinger.

"Forty-three degrees north, seventy-six degrees west, sir," reported B-5.

"Buzz on," commanded B-1, and the entire swarm flew off on a mission.

"What was that?" asked Humphrey.

"THE WAGGLE DANCE. It's how honeybees communicate

where the best pollen can be found," answered Stan.

"But they are bears. Rainbow-colored bears," stated Sam.

"WE MUST BE HONEY BEARS!" cheered the bears, and they started to do the dance again but were quickly stopped.

"I've had enough of this!" said

Mayor Quill. "By Mayoral Decree one-two-three-six—"

"Actually, one-two-three-seven, sir. Mayoral Decree one-two-three-six is 'Honey for everyone,'" corrected Humphrey.

"By Mayoral Decree number one thousand two hundred thirty-SIX, there are to be NO WAGGLE DANCING and NO HONEY and NO BEES in the Grumpy Woods!" And with that declaration, Mayor Quill stomped his foot. He shook from head to toe. He tightened his grip on the honey bottle. Humphrey rolled into a defensive ball. Honey squirted everywhere.

CHAPTER EIGHT

Sure enough, the swarm returned from forty-three degrees north, seventy-six degrees west with plenty of pollen. So much so that the production of the hive was soon beyond capacity. New, smaller hives popped up everywhere along the wall.

Other squadrons, who'd heard of Queen Beetrice's success, flew in from nearby. Everyone wanted to be a part of the honey empire.

As the bees produced more and more honey, the bears were having trouble keeping up. A bear can only guzzle so much honey, or so they

learned. And with the recent boycott placed on honey, no one *except* the bears was permitted to eat it.

Stan organized a team of door-to-door salesbees, who attempted to sell to the townscritters but were met with slamming door after slamming door.

The bees quickly ran out of squeezy bear bottles and began

filling every jar, bucket, and satchel
the bears could get their paws on.
Those ran out quickly, too. Soon
honey dripped, pooled, and oozed
over every inch of the woods.

Mayor Quill held a meeting in the
trees above City Hall. The hall itself
was a tad too sticky at the moment.

The townscritters came with their complaints. Some even held signs protesting the misspoken Mayoral Decree 1,236.

"WhooOOO can sleep with all of yooOOOu roaming through my tree all day long?" screeched Opal Owl.

"We explained that, Opal," said Humphrey. "The only safe way to

navigate the Grumpy Woods at
the present time is through the
treetops. We're just lucky that
most of us can climb." And then
he quickly added, "Sorry, Dawn,"
to Dawn Fawn, who was grounded.
For a neat freak such as Dawn, that
was pure torture.

"Icky sticky! Icky
sticky! Icky sticky!"
Dawn sang on repeat.

Then Dawn caught a
glimpse of Bernice in one
of the lower branches and

shrieked, "I NEED
MY DUST BUNNY!"
Before Bernice could
react, Dawn hopped
up and snatched
the bunny in
her mouth.
Then she tried
to use Bernice's
fuzzy tush to sop up a
river of honey flowing
down the tree trunk.
Unfortunately, this only

resulted in Bernice becoming stuck to the tree.

"You didn't hear this from me, but maybe we need to lift the boycott on honey," suggested Sam. He really wanted to try eating nuts and honey together. Sam was a sucker for salty-sweet snacks.

"Absolutely not!" said Mayor Quill. "If we start eating the honey,

what message does that send? That
the bees have a home here in the
woods?"

"However," said Humphrey, "a
dozen bears can only eat so much
honey. Too bad we don't have *more*
Super Happy Party Bears."

Everyone just stared at
Humphrey.

"Preposterous!" yelled Mayor
Quill.

The awkward silence continued
until it was broken by Sam, who
had scurried away unnoticed and
was now scurrying back.

"You are never going to believe
what I just saw!" said Sam. He had a
dollop of honey on his furry cheek
and was licking something off his
claws. It was no secret what he
had been up to. He had eaten some
honey! "Come quick!"

103

Sam led the group. Opal flew above the tree line. Dawn, having finally pried Bernice from the tree trunk, traveled below with the bunny in her mouth. Sherry rode on Dawn's back. Mayor Quill and Humphrey followed slowly behind Sam over branches and in between twisted limbs. And of course there was bickering.

"Stop pushing!"

"Don't bounce so much!"

"Get off my tail!"

When they arrived at the Grumpy Wall, the townscritters

were shocked at what they found.
Amid all the honey-flavored chaos
was a big, furry pile of Super Happy
Sleeping Bears.

CHAPTER NINE

The townscritters never thought
the Super Happy Party Bears could
be so still or so quiet, but there
they were. The only movement
came from their rising and falling
bellies. The only sound was a faint
snoring that vaguely seemed to

mimic "If You're Happy and You Know It."

"Welcome!" a voice rang out from the wall. It was Stan. "New customers!"

"What happened to them?" asked Mayor Quill, pointing to the snoozing bears.

"Um, one second they were

guzzling honey, and the next
second they were sound asleep.
Personally, I think it is just a good
ol'-fashioned sugar crash. But they
called it hibernation."

"Hibernation?!" shrieked Sam,
his face now incredibly sticky
with the honey he'd secretly been
eating. "Is it winter? I need to store

more nuts. I feel a chill. Is that a snowflake?" Sam ran in circles, panicking. Then all the sugar from the honey overwhelmed him, and he crashed right into the heap of bears.

"Cute little fella," said Stan, pushing his glasses back up on his nose. "Now, what can I get you fine folks? A honey chew? Toast with honey? Or our original Super Happy Party Bear honey-glazed doughnut? It's a collaborative effort we're quite proud of here at Beetrice's Honey Hive."

"We do not want honey," said Mayor Quill. "What we want is for you and your hive to pack up and get out of the Grumpy Woods. Your sticky stuff is not welcome here."

"Well said, sir." Humphrey applauded the mayor. And then to Stan, "We don't want you sticking around!"

"And clean up this messss," added Sherry.

"I understand you have concerns," said Stan. "Here is the number for our customer service

To file a complaint, call
1-800-BUZZ-OFF

department, where you can file a complaint."

"File a complaint?" said Mayor Quill. "Why can't I just talk to you?"

"We outsourced our customer service. Queen Beetrice figured it would help us focus on production and distribution. Please allow two to three weeks for a response," explained Stan, and with that, he flew away.

The townscritters were baffled. If the bees kept making honey, someone needed to eat it all up before it flooded the whole forest. There was only one thing to do.

"I think we need to eat the honey," said Bernice.

"Now, wait a minute, Honey Bunny! There is an official boycott by decree of the mayor," Humphrey reminded them.

"But if *we* can't eat the honey,
who will?" asked Bernice.

"I have a plan," said Humphrey.
"You see, bears hibernate when the
temperature drops and
winter arrives. They
wake up only in
spring, when it
gets warmer."

"But it's spring right now," said Opal. "I hardly see how that is helpful information."

"Let'ssss raisssse the temperature," said Sherry.

The townscritters got to work doing just that. They covered the bears with quilts. They built a bonfire. It was really cozy. The bears still snoozed.

"I don't believe this," said Mayor Quill. "I always wished the bears

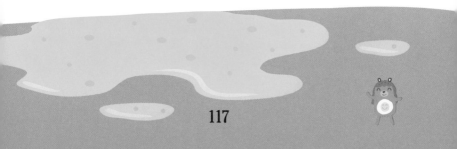

117

would have a slumber party and be quiet for once, and now that they are slumbering, all I want to do is wake them up!"

"We need to have an *un*-slumber party," suggested Humphrey.

Everyone grumbled about it, but no one had a better idea, so they got to work. First stop: the Party Patch, for the necessary party supplies.

The townscritters soon returned
to the Grumpy Wall with party in
hand.

"This had better work,"
mumbled Mayor Quill.

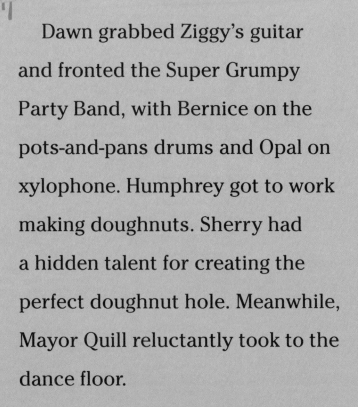

Dawn grabbed Ziggy's guitar and fronted the Super Grumpy Party Band, with Bernice on the pots-and-pans drums and Opal on xylophone. Humphrey got to work making doughnuts. Sherry had a hidden talent for creating the perfect doughnut hole. Meanwhile, Mayor Quill reluctantly took to the dance floor.

"Was it hop to the right; slide

to the left; shimmy, shake, shake; strike a pose? Or slide to the left; shake to the right; hoppy, shimmy, shake; strike a pose?" As Mayor Quill struggled to find his party rhythm, there was a stirring in the sleepy heap.

The littlest bear lifted his head and yawned. "Quilly is dancing!" And with that, hibernation ended and the bears woke up.

CHAPTER TEN

"IT'S SUPER HAPPY PARTY TIME!

SUPER HAPPY PARTY TIME!"

cheered the bears as they woke up

to join Mayor Quill on the dance

floor and swiftly placed a glass of honey in his paw.

"I know a party game we can play," said Mayor Quill loudly over the music. "Who can eat the most honey in the next five minutes?!"

"WE LOVE HONEY!" cheered the bears. They were playing right into Mayor Quill's plan to clean up the Grumpy Woods.

"On your mark, get set, GO!" said Mayor Quill.

The bears tore through the woods. They licked the tree trunks. They slurped up the puddles. Soon there wasn't a drop left. Everything was sparkly clean.

"That was fun!" squealed

the bears. "MORE HONEY!
MORE HONEY!"

The littlest bear knocked on the tiny hive door, but there was no answer. The hive was quiet. Not a bee in sight.

Just then Queen Beetrice

appeared, followed by a worker

bee carrying suitcases. Suddenly, a

whole swarm of bees surrounded

her. Some bees even had a camera

and a notepad.

"Your Majesty, I'm Wax Stinger

from *Buzzworthy News*. Care to
make a statement?" said one
reporter bee with a microphone.

"This market is just too
unpredictable. One minute we're
the bee's knees. The next

moment no one's buying. We're moving shop."

"Where will you go?" asked another reporter.

"Somewhere a *little less unstable*," said Queen Beetrice while glaring at the townscritters. "B-1! Let's buzz off!" And at that command, the swarm formed the shape of a helicopter. As Queen Beetrice turned to leave, she waved one last time to her adoring crowd before the hum of the bee propellers carried her away.

"We didn't get to say good-bye

to Stan," said
the littlest
bear.

"How
sad," said
Mops.

"I'm going to
miss him," said
Jigs.

"And our doughnut
collaboration," added Jacks.

"Did someone say 'doughnuts'?"
asked Stan.

"STAN!!!" cheered the bears. "We
thought you left."

"Yes. We thought you left," said Humphrey sternly. "You'd better hurry up and leave."

"I decided to stay," said Stan. "But don't worry. There won't be any more mess or pesky squadrons. I set up a Getsy shop online. So we'll just get a few deliveries every now and then. All the messy work is done elsewhere."

"SUPER HAPPY HONEY TIME!" the bears cheered.

And they did their Super Happy Party Dance. Slide to the right. Hop

131

to the left. Shimmy, shimmy, shake.

Strike a pose.

Stan passed out honey-glazed
doughnuts with an extra squeeze of
honey.

The townscritters ate some honey, too. Mayor Quill decided to look the other way.

They were feeling just a *little* less grumpy.

ABOUT THE AUTHOR

In previous chapters, Marcie Colleen has been a teacher, an actress, and a nanny, but now she spends her days writing children's books! She lives in her very own Party Patch, Headquarters of Fun, with her husband and their mischievous sock monkey in San Diego, California. Occasionally, there are even doughnuts. This is her first chapter book series.

Don't Miss the other ☀ SUPER HAPPY PARTY BEARS Books